Immortal Curse Series Illustrated Edition Volume One

Based on the world created by
USA Today Bestselling Author

Lexi C. Foss

Coloring Pages Illustrated by

Arnild C. Aldepolla

Colored Illustrations by

Keni Aryani

Immortal Curse Series: Illustrated Edition
Volume One

Editing by: Outthink Editing, LLC

Cover Design by: Julie Nicholls with JMN Art/Covers by Julie

Coloring Book Page Illustrations by: Arnild C. Aldepolla

Colored Illustrations by Keni Aryani

Published by: Ninja Newt Publishing, LLC

Print Edition
ISBN: 978-1-950694-92-1

This is for the Immortal Curse fans. Thank you for loving this world as much as I do.

Hugs,
Lexi

LEXI C. FOSS
ILLUSTRATED BY ARNILD C. ALDEPOLLA
Immortal Curse Series
THE ADULT COLORING BOOK
VOL. 1

BLOOD
LAWS

"An unknown power is surfacing. She will possess the strength and will to destroy us all unless certain measures are put in place to curb her inclinations."

–Prophetess Skye

Stas couldn't blink. Couldn't move. Couldn't think.

It had finally happened.

The supernaturals had found her.

She needed to fight, to flee, but her limbs refused her. There wasn't any point.

Because she stood no chance, just like her parents that day.

This is my ending, not my beginning.

Today is the day I die.

"Dating for information," Issac whispered. "A simple quid pro quo situation. You help me and I'll help you."

"How is our pretending to date going to help you?"

The devil grinned in his gaze. "Does the why really matter when I have the answers you seek?"

Did it? Stas wasn't sure. "If I agree, will you tell me what I am?"

"Hmm." His attention drifted to her mouth, his pupils flaring. "I will after our first date."

"She knows Jonathan," Lucian said, scratching the blond stubble dotting his chin. "Which can only mean one thing. You're using the girl to get vengeance for Amelia."

"I am." The words tasted bitter in Issac's mouth, mainly because he felt responsible for her current situation. He only meant to pique Jonathan's interest. Which he clearly succeeded in doing since the lunatic tried to poison the poor woman.

"But she's a fledgling," Lucian added.

"Yes," he confirmed, aware of what the Hydraian King really wanted to know. Fledglings were rare, and one as powerful as Astasiya was even rarer. "In addition to being resistant to psychic gifts, she has a persuasive talent."

"Are you trying to make a deal with me, Miss Davenport?"

Fierce green eyes met his, provoking all manner of inappropriate thoughts. Like what they would look like in the throes of passion. "No, I'm giving you my terms."

Issac nearly laughed.

No woman ever gave him terms for a date.

Not that this necessarily qualified since he considered it more of a business arrangement.

They needed to be seen in public together for his plan to work, and to put to rest any suspicions the CRF had about her reacting to the Nizari poison. Winning her over in the process would be an added bonus, one that would make her more helpful.

"We've already gone over the part about me not being a socialite. Besides, we're not really dating."

"No?" It certainly felt like they were. At least tonight. His thumb slipped beneath the silk, lightly brushing her inner thigh.

"No, it's a business deal. Although, I really don't know what you're getting out of it."

He leaned in closer, his palm sliding up her leg. Her shuddering breath fanned his lips. "Are you sure about that, Astasiya?"

"Who told you to come here, Astasiya?"

"Why do you care?" she countered, her voice higher than she intended. He evoked a response from her unlike any other. Not that her limited experience was much of a comparison.

"Because whoever sent you here is trying to get you killed."

"I need to bite you," Issac whispered. "To mark you as mine to protect you."

Astasiya swallowed, her hesitation palpable. After a beat, she breathed, "Okay."

His incisors ached from that one word alone, her blood so close, so potent, so *perfect*. He sank his teeth into her skin, breaking the surface swiftly and efficiently and eliciting a sharp squeak of protest from her throat. It was quickly replaced by a heady moan as he unleashed the endorphins into her bloodstream—a mechanism used by Ichorian kind to help subdue their prey.

Astasiya's arms tightened around him, her lower body arching and seeking purpose against his cock.

ARCADIA

I'm surrounded by demons.

The same demons who may have killed Owen.

The same demons who did *kill my parents.*

Oh God…

Was the culprit here? The man with the gold-flecked black eyes?

Her heart stopped.

What if he recognized her?

What if someone here knew about her friendship with Owen?

She'd end up in that chair, the throne in the center of the room.

"Mortals who overreact die, and they die badly."

"Do you understand why Lucian is here?" Issac continued, not giving her a chance to speak. "The danger you were in last night, well, let's just say I haven't felt that way in a very long time. That's why I called Lucian. He's here to help you become a Hydraian and to help keep you alive."

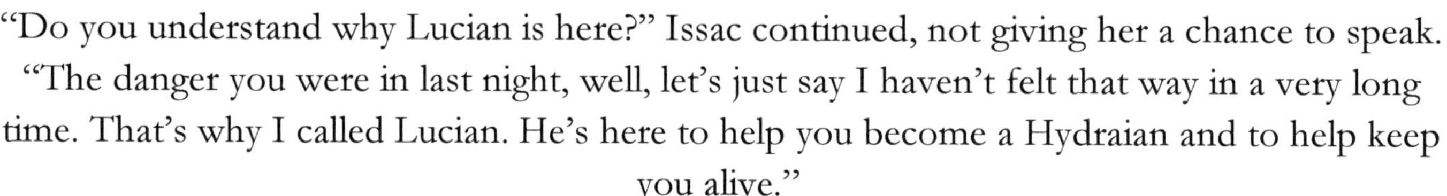

Stas bit the inside of her cheek. That's what he meant about her packing a few things, but he phrased it as a choice. Like she *might* decide to leave. "But what about your revenge?" That was the whole point of their association.

He palmed the back of his neck. "It seems my desire for you to live trumps my need to avenge my sister's murder."

He opened the drawer of the dresser beside them and pulled out a pair of swim trunks. She frowned at it. Storing swimwear in the pool house made sense, but there were other clothes beside it.

Issac took several steps toward the door before pausing, not meeting her gaze. "I'm going for a swim. Let me know if I need to find somewhere else to sleep tonight. I'll understand if you need space."

"How does it feel to not be able to touch something you want, Aya? Does it burn you the way it burned me?"

She shivered at the possessive hold and nipped his bottom lip in protest. "I could command you to let me go," she said, her voice drowsy with lust.

"But that requires you to have a voice." His mouth covered hers, taking her slowly, making his point clear. His free hand returned to her breast before drifting down toward the sweet spot between her thighs. He found her clit through the fabric, pressing it with his thumb.

She cried out against his lips, evoking a grin from him.

"Try commanding me now, little fledgling." His teasing tone made her want to do just that, but he distracted her by rolling the pad of his thumb in a sensuous circle, her hips bucking in response.

"Now, Tom just mentioned you met Osiris," Doctor Fitzgerald continued, curiosity coloring his tone. "I'm afraid that makes it a little more imperative for you to join us. If you become a Sentinel, I can give you certain resources that are not available to civilians—resources that can save your life."

Well, that was unexpected. "You can protect me from Osiris?"

"I can provide you with the ability to guard yourself, yes."

"Like weapons?" she guessed.

"Among other things." He laced his fingers together on the table again, leaning toward her conspiratorially. "I'm sure Issac has promised to keep you safe, but his way would involve taking on immortality. Am I right?"

Not in the way you think, she thought while nodding.

"That's a big decision. Are you ready to make it?"

CRF
CATASTROPHIC
RELIEF FOUNDATION

Forbidden Bonds

"Amelia," Tom's deep voice rumbled, "this isn't a dream."

"What?"

"You're not dreaming."

She smiled and shook her head. Of course she was dreaming. What else could this be? There was water, sunshine, and trees. "I wish for you to go now." No need for the handsome Sentinel to spoil her temporary reprieve from reality.

"I wish I could, but I'm stuck here for the foreseeable future." Tom rose to his full height beside her and held out a hand. "Let's get back to the cabin. You need a shower, and I need to get some sleep."

A woodsy scent assaulted her senses as he wrapped his arms around her from behind and took hold of her wrists. This was not at all how she expected a man to smell or feel after exercising without a shower. The earthy undertone was actually quite pleasant, if a little distracting.

"Gun in your right hand. Good. Now you're going to lock your right arm like this." He demonstrated by pulling it straight and locking her elbow. "Lower your head a little so your line of sight is focused on the target." He slid a hand to her bicep on the other side. "Left arm, not as tight. You want a slight bend in your elbow. Your right arm will control the recoil."

"Recoil?" she repeated as he pressed his body tight against her back. *Why does that feel so good?*

"You'll understand in a minute." He curled her finger around the trigger and swiveled her hips a bit to the right. "Do you see the target there? Down the center of the barrel?" His breath was hot against her ear, making her shiver.

It took more effort than it should to focus on the bull's-eye. "I see it." Hitting it would be another matter.

"Okay, straddle me again."

This woman is trying to kill me, Tom thought.

The first few days of training were a breeze because they kept the touching to a minimum. He taught Amelia the weak points on the shin, how to properly form a punch, and general self-defense basics. Today, they graduated to full-body contact.

Why am I doing this to myself? he wondered—not for the first time—as he straddled Amelia's hips. This had gone beyond a death wish and firmly into torture territory. What had started as a fun way to pass the time had escalated to a risky activity that required too much skin-on-skin contact.

"Hold me down like you mean it," Amelia chided when he gently placed his hands on her shoulders. "No going easy on me."

"Keep your legs spread, arms above your head." Tom's commanding tone showered goose bumps down her limbs, and not the good kind. She met his cool gaze with one of her own and lifted her arms as requested. His betrayal hurt, but she wouldn't give him the satisfaction of knowing that.

Warmth spread up her side as his palms ran from her waist to the sides of her breasts. Unlike Scott, he didn't take any liberties but kept it light and professional. His fingers trailed down the center of her sternum to her abdomen before running over the front of her thighs.

She shivered when he told her to face the house. The heat from his body confused her senses, as did the seductive hint of pine teasing her nostrils. *I cannot still be attracted to him. Not after everything.*

"Remember what I told you?" His words were a breath against her ear, so low she barely heard him. "Element of surprise, sweetheart."

Exhaustion took over, making her eyes droop and her limbs heavy.

She didn't want to ever move, but Tom seemed to have other ideas as he reached over to turn off the shower and wrapped her in a towel.

It all happened in a daze. She barely registered him carrying her to the bed but recognized his familiar warmth when he returned. His wet clothes were gone and replaced by a dry shirt and boxers. She rolled toward him on instinct and sighed when his arms settled around her.

"I'm so going to hell," he muttered.

"I'll welcome the company," she replied with a yawn. Hell was her reality for the last six or so years. If he wanted to join her, she wouldn't turn him away.

He snorted. "Get some sleep, Amelia."

"Do it," Tom whispered, startling her. She met his wary gaze and felt a piece of her heart break. Witnessing the resignation in his gaze was too much. When he grabbed her shoulder to draw her closer, she went because she couldn't fight him. Not like this. His opposite hand wrapped around her wrist, but instead of disarming her, he guided the barrel to his rib cage.

"Shoot me," he urged. "If it's what you need to do, then do it."

A tear found its way to the corner of her eye and rolled down her cheek. She couldn't remember the last time she cried; she thought Jonathan had beaten it out of her.

The palm on her shoulder slid to the back of her neck as Tom pulled her down the rest of the way and rolled her beneath him. His grip on her wrist never faltered as he kept the gun aimed at his chest. She shuddered as his hips settled between her legs, and closed her eyes when his lips brushed hers.

"I'll understand, Amelia. I know it's what I deserve."

"Tell me you want this," Tom breathed. "I need to know you want this, sweetheart." Her heart fluttered in response to the endearment. She loved the way it rolled off his lips onto hers.

Amelia tried to capture his mouth again, only to be held down by the palm between her breasts. His eyes smoldered with an intensity that caused her pulse to race. Arousal never looked so good on a man. And she thought he didn't want her. *What was I thinking?*

"Kiss me," she pleaded. "I need you to kiss me."

"I want to do a lot more than kiss you, Amelia." The warning in his voice made her shiver.

She swallowed. "Then do it."

"One word, and I stop. Say no, and it all stops."

Never. "Kiss me," she repeated. "Please."

"I want to taste every inch of you," he whispered against her lips. He led with his tongue, taking her mouth with a possessiveness that left her breathless.

"You cannot possibly expect me to get on that thing," she blurted out as the man behind the desk watched with a wrinkly brow.

Just stealing a bike, kid. Nothing to see here.

"I do," Tom replied. "Hop on."

Her head swung back and forth. "Absolutely not."

"Seriously? After everything we've gone through, a bike is what you take issue with?" Didn't they just agree not to bicker until they were safe?

"It's a death trap."

"And standing here arguing while a horde of Ichorians are searching for us isn't?" he asked, baffled.

She bit her lip and shook her head again.

Stubborn woman. "Here." Tom held out the helmet, and she cocked a challenging brow in response. They didn't have time for this. "Put this on, and get on the bike. We've gotta go. Now."

"I'd prefer a car" was her succinct reply.

"And I'd prefer to get the hell out of here. Put on the damn helmet, Amelia."

"You also make me feel strong," she told him. "In addition to the peace and comfort, I mean."

"Yeah?"

She nodded. "And you teach me things. It may have been a diversion at first, but I think you enjoyed training me."

His grin was automatic. "Oh, I more than enjoyed it." He fucking loved it.

"What did you enjoy most?" she asked, a smile in her voice. So much better than the sadness lurking there before. He liked playing with flirtatious Amelia.

"Everything." From the gun stance lessons to rolling around with her on the ground, he enjoyed every minute. If he died soon, those would be the memories he'd miss most. And their one explosive night together.

Well, this isn't awkward at all.

Three sets of eyes stared down at him, only one of them making him truly uncomfortable. "Stas," he greeted.

Her wide gaze swung back and forth between him and Amelia. Then understanding colored her expression, and she jumped in front of her fuming boyfriend. "Issac, don't."

"As if I could," Wakefield seethed. "This is not cute, Amelia."

Tom frowned at his harsh tone. "Don't talk to her like that," he said at the same time someone else said something very similar in his voice. He glanced to his left and met the gaze of his identical twin. *Holy shit.* "You shifted."

"Nice try, sweetheart," Amelia replied in a voice that sounded exactly like his own. "She doesn't need to see this, Wakefield. Take her away."

Tom gaped at her, then realized what she was doing. "Oh, hell no. She's lying."

His identical twin rolled his eyes. *Note to self: never roll my eyes again because I look like an idiot.* "Give me a gun, and I'll prove who's lying."

"You know what else I didn't feel before you?"

She shook her head. "No. What?"

He nibbled her earlobe and whispered, "Love."

"And you feel that now?"

He nodded. "For you, I do."

Her smile took his breath away. "Truly?"

"Truly," he repeated with a grin. Her accent amused him, especially when she used odd words like *truly*. He tucked a damp strand behind her ear and allowed some seriousness to leak through. Actions were his preference over spoken endearments, but there were some moments that required words, and this was one of them.

"You make me feel, Amelia. You're my home."

BLOOD
HEART

Abs.

That was the first thought that registered.

Because the man had greeted her shirtless.

A pair of navy gym shorts sat low on his lean hips, leaving his muscular physique on full display. The trail of moisture licking a path over his chiseled chest suggested he'd been working out. At least that explained the clanking and banging.

"Um…" Lizzie met a pair of soft brown eyes and faltered.

Milk chocolate, her cook's brain supplied.

I don't care what color they are, she snapped back.

Or that his gaze appeared to be roaming shamelessly over her body right now.

No.

Focus.

We're here to yell.

Right.

She cleared her throat and leveled the attractive man with a look she used on her misbehaving students. "I live in the condo beneath yours, and your—uh—workout, is, well, it's distracting me from my work."

"Beautiful," the Ichorian murmured. "I'll be keeping these since you just destroyed my favorite pistol."

"Perhaps you shouldn't have fired it at me," Jayson growled.

The uninvited visitor stood to his full height. "I had to ensure you were still a worthy opponent, and you proved as qualified as ever, Jedrick."

God, that name. Jayson hadn't heard it in over a millennium. "I go by Jayson now, or Jay."

The black-haired immortal shut the front door before leaning against it and folding his lean arms. "Really? Why?"

"You don't ever change your name, *Ezekiel?*"

He laughed. "Actually, it's Kiel right now."

"Kiel," Jayson repeated. "Like *kill?*"

"A brilliant play on words, no? Can't say the same about Jayson. A bit boring, if you ask me."

"Okay, a Nizari assassin told Jayson he knows about me, but he hasn't done anything yet. Is it because he doesn't suspect me, or is it something else?"

"Ezekiel's intentions are cryptic at best, but he's notorious for playing with his food." The Ichorian was renowned for his cruelty and lethal intelligence. His ability to track by blood type increased his notoriety. He was part of the short list of beings Issac considered to be a true threat.

"But he hasn't come after me yet," she repeated.

He arched a brow. "And so you would prefer to wait for such a moment?"

"Is the coffee in Greece better?"

"It is."

"Which you know because you've lived there?" She kept the question light and innocent, not letting on to how much she truly wanted the answer.

But he saw right through it.

"Oh, Red." His arm fell to her shoulders as he leaned into her personal space. "I believe you owe me cookies first."

"I didn't know when you would be back." A sad excuse since she never intended to bake them anyway, but he didn't know that.

"Uh-huh. You could have called to ask."

"And you could have texted me at any point to say hello, but you didn't."

His chuckle was low and sexy, and far too intimate. "So what you're saying is, if I want cookies, I need to message you?"

Coffee Latt
FRAPUCCINO

Balthazar released Lizzie's hand far too slowly for Jayson's liking as he asked, "I assume you're staying for the party?"

"Party?" she repeated.

What are you doing?

Shh. I've got this, Jay, his eyes seemed to say.

Oh, I bet you do.

"Jay didn't tell you?" Balthazar tsked. "That's just like him. He doesn't know how to properly host." That last part was whispered conspiratorially at Lizzie, eliciting a giggle from her.

Now you're just being a dick.

Balthazar's gaze glimmered deviously. "Like even now, he still hasn't offered you a drink." He shook his head in mock reproach. "What can I get you, sweetheart? A glass of wine, perhaps?"

She slid her hands up his arms, luxuriating in the Italian silk of his blazer. Lizzie adored the sleek and sexy look, and Jayson wore it so well. She traced the collar of his shirt before dragging her nails up his neck and into his luscious hair.

All their previous kisses were controlled by him, but she desired more.

She locked her fingers in his thick strands and leaned into him.

"Stop teasing and kiss me," she demanded. The voice sounded nothing like hers—so throaty and hot—but it inspired the reaction she wanted.

"Careful what you wish for, Red." He lifted her onto the island counter, yanked her forward, and stepped between her thighs. "You just might get it."

GRAPE

"What are you doing to me?" she asked with a groan.

"Prolonging the moment," he replied, tilting his head to the side with a knowing smile. "Trust me. You'll thank me for it later."

"Right now, I want to kill you."

"No, sweetheart. You want to fuck me. I can see how you might confuse the two, but they're unrelated." He finished removing his button-down and the fitted shirt beneath; and began loosening his belt.

Her lips fell open at the implication, causing him to pause, but she didn't have it in her to tell him to stop. How could she turn down a naked Jayson?

Blood? Gross.

"Like a vampire?" It came out as a squeak.

He chuckled. "A myth, I assure you, but a similar concept. Try not to use that term too loudly outside our glass walls, though, darling. My kind do not take lightly to being compared to vile creatures of the night—our ancestry is much lighter."

Lizzie gripped the edge of her seat. "You're… This is… impossible. It's not…" She shook her head as she frantically tried to clear it. "I can't…"

Vampires aren't real. The supernatural isn't real.

"I can bring Cynthia in for a demonstration, if you'd like." He sounded so reasonable and normal, like he spoke about immortality and vampires on a daily basis. "Or you could peek over your shoulder into the booth below us near the dance floor, but if you could keep the screaming to a minimum, my ears would thank you for it."

He answered his phone as it started to vibrate. "Talk to me, M."

"Do you have your American passport handy?"

Jayson frowned. "No. It's in the condo."

"Okay. I suggest you ask Jacque to pop over and retrieve it for you because you're running out of time." A ding popped on Jayson's phone while Mateo was talking. "Congratulations. You've just been booked on the last available *Polaris Business* seat to Rome, and your flight leaves in sixty-seven minutes."

"Tell me the seat is next to hers," he growled.

"Of course. Safe travels, Jay."

MAGAZINE
Babelart
15/10/20

"Sorry, Red," he murmured, easing his hold. He'd grabbed her harder than he meant to—a reaction to the approaching weapons. "We need to go."

"H-how do you know—"

"Guns," he replied quickly. "Now follow me." He grasped her hand and tugged her toward a side exit that was clearly not part of the original architecture.

His ability continued to scan for metal associated with gun power as he pulled a phone from his pocket. He'd texted Luc with an update when they arrived and also sent a message to Jacque to remain on standby.

Jayson had suspected the CRF would arrive and ruin their little field trip at some point, hence the necessary backup plan.

Jacque picked up on the first ring. "Yo."

"The CRF found us," he explained as Lizzie sputtered beside him. "We need a teleport. Now. Get B and have him explain to you where the *apodyterium* is located. He has fond memories of that place."

"Why are you hiding?" he asked, voice deceptively soft. The heat from his chest radiated against hers, but he didn't touch her. Not physically, anyway.

"I-I'm not."

He traced the top of the towel, just over her breasts. "Liar."

Jayson tugged on the knot, and her hands flew up to catch the fabric before it fell. Butterflies took flight in her abdomen as he grinned at her instinctual reaction.

"I warned you, Red." A sharp yank sent the towel to the floor. "I'm done holding back."

Lizzie tried to cover herself, but he captured her wrists and pressed them against the wall on either side of her head. Warmth pooled between her legs at the show of dominance, causing her to squirm and Jayson to grin.

His gaze touched every inch of her bare skin, leaving her hot and bothered by the end of his exploration.

"This color looks amazing on you." Approval deepened his tone, sending a shiver down her spine despite the warm air. "I think we're ready to renegotiate limits."

"I think we should play a game and find out just how far this infatuation goes," he mused. "Would you like that, Lizzie? To learn Jay's true feelings?"

"Do we have time for that, sir?" Stark asked, an edge to his tone that wasn't reflected in his bored expression.

"Of course. Why else did we come prepared?"

"Because we assumed he would be here, sir."

"And I suspect he will be any moment now." John touched his ear. "Any sign of the Elder?"

"You died, Aya." Three words, uttered so softly she almost didn't hear them. Or maybe that was the wind tunnel suddenly taking residence in her head that distorted the sound.

"What?" She couldn't have heard him right.

"You went to Bora Bora by yourself—without backup—and were shot in the head."

She blinked as the memory began to surface. So lost in her nightmare, she hadn't realized the truth of the moment.

"John," she breathed. "Where's…?" Her voice faltered.

Oh, fuck.

No.

No way.

This can't…

"I…" She released his wrist to feel her forehead and found nothing but smooth skin.

Her heart stuttered as her breath caught in her throat.

I died.

Ezekiel smirked. "Elizabeth is a key reason for our meeting tonight, yes. She's one of a kind, and Osiris would like her back."

"Over my dead body," Jayson growled.

"That can certainly be arranged," Ezekiel murmured as Osiris tapped him on the arm. They exchanged a long look that left the assassin grinning. "It appears my Sire has decided to grant her freedom. For now."

"For now?" Stas repeated. "What the hell does that mean?"

"I believe his objective has shifted, little angel." His gold-flecked gaze sparkled. "You are quite the enigma, darling one. And he's intrigued."

Ice dotted her spine as she interpreted his meaning. "I'm his new objective."

"Oh God, Jayson." She shook her head as more tears rolled down her pink cheeks. "No, that's not a no… hold on… I'm just… oh my God, I've gone and screwed it up already." She laughed and shook her head again. "Crap!"

Her face reddened even more, which he found both adorable and infuriating. The latter only because he wanted to kiss her, but he couldn't while she was still deciding how to respond.

She took a steadying breath, her hands gripping his harder than she probably realized. After several agonizing seconds, she finally met his gaze again and smiled.

"Yes," she said, her eyes matching the word. "Of course, yes. Always, yes. I… I don't even know where to start, but yes. I would love to marry you."

BLOOD
BONDS

"Seraphim do not indulge in pleasures of the flesh. It is a human tradition that holds no value to eternal beings."

–Caro

"What do you say, angel?" he whispered, his lips brushing hers. "I'll give you the information you need in exchange for a night in my bed. Does that sound practical enough to you?"

Ezekiel snatched the mug and slammed it down on the counter. "Skye prophesied Osiris's demise, and it involves you and some unknown entity."

Sethios blinked at his oldest friend. "What?"

"He's already on his way here. We need to go. Now." Ezekiel reached for him just as Caro walked out wearing Sethios's clothes. "Fuck."

His best friend whipped out a knife and threw it without blinking an eye. The metal glinted in the early afternoon sunlight streaming through the windows as the sharp edge sailed toward Caro's head.

Sethios didn't think. He just reacted.

Mist to me. The command hit her faster than the blade, forcing her to shift to his side. Caro stumbled into him, and he caught her with his arm.

Ezekiel gaped at them, his eyebrows shooting upward. "Well, hello, unknown entity." Those gold-flecked eyes radiated awe. "A Seraphim?"

"Pretty, isn't she?" Amusement touched Sethios's chest as Caro growled at his diminutive tone. "And please don't kill her, E. I'm not done playing."

"What did the seers say about my purpose?" she asked, returning the conversation back to something pertinent.

"You were never meant to complete your assignment. Sethios was your target all along." His green gaze lifted to the man holding her. "Your child represents a future possibility the seers wish to see fulfilled."

"The unknown entity," Sethios whispered, his expression morphing into one of awe and skepticism. "But how is that possible? I've fucked numerous women over my lifetime—so many that I've lost count. None of them have ever fallen pregnant."

"Caro is a full-blooded Seraphim, and it seems your genetics were a perfect match for breeding."

"A team," she repeated. "And if I would prefer to be in the sanctuary of my own people?"

"The same beings who sent you on a bogus errand with the intention of impregnating you with my child?" He smirked. "If that's your desire, then I'll either follow you or do what I can to protect you from here. But I would request—beg, even—that you wait to decide until after we know more about the prophecy."

Her lips threatened to curl. "Beg?" She might enjoy seeing that.

His gaze narrowed. "This is a serious conversation."

"Yes," she agreed. "You begging is very serious to me."

"Now you're teasing me," he growled, wrapping his hands around her wrists. "I'm trying to discuss something important, and you're smiling."

"I'm not smiling."

"Your eyes are smiling." He moved closer, sliding between her legs and lowering her palms to the armrests of the chair. "You know what I think?"

She bit her lip and shook her head. Though, she had an idea of where he might be headed given the devilish glint in his dark green eyes.

"I think you like me," he replied. "In fact, I think you might even find me useful during this pregnancy."

Her eyebrows rose. "In what way?"

"Hot chocolate, for one." His fingers slid from her wrists to her knees and started exploring upward beneath her dress. "I can also offer pleasure, something I hear pregnant women fancy."

"I don't work for anyone."

"A partnership, then."

"I don't work *with* anyone either."

"I see." The light dimmed in Ezekiel's gaze, darkening his irises to a near black. "In that case, you don't need me, do you?"

Well played, Ichorian. Well played.

"What are you requesting in return for your assistance?" Gabriel didn't want to beat around the bush or continue this posturing game. He wanted to arrive at the point and be done with all the prophecy business.

Then he might return to take a second look at the CRF.

"I'm not sure yet. It depends on how good you are, Stark."

Gabriel frowned. "Stark?"

"Consider it a nickname. Keeps me from knowing your real identity and it suits you." The Ichorian winked. "I assume you've already tried to enter Osiris's estate and failed?"

"Entering was not my issue so much as locating my target."

"And what do you intend to do with your 'target'?"

"Request a prophecy. Nothing more. Nothing less."

CRF
CATASTROPHIC
RELIEF FOUNDATI

"Wandering that maze is Skye's favorite outdoor activity. Osiris grants her one hour a day outside—unaccompanied—and she always ventures there."

Interesting. "He doesn't worry that she'll use that time to try to escape?" Because Gabriel would use it to his advantage in that situation.

"No. She can't leave."

"Can't or won't?" There was a distinct difference.

"Can't."

"Because Osiris has compelled her to stay," Gabriel inferred. "There has to be a way to break it."

Ezekiel's dark eyes held his. "If you know of one, I would give you anything in return for that knowledge."

"Noted," Gabriel murmured. Ezekiel could prove useful to him, especially if he wanted to learn more about the CRF. It would be prudent to exchange information, and helping him thwart Osiris wouldn't be a hardship. "What if someone forces her to leave?" he asked, curious. "Wouldn't that make her unwilling and thereby trick the compulsion?" From what Gabriel understood, persuasion was specific, not ambiguous.

Ezekiel didn't appear fazed by the notion. If anything, his gaze glittered with memories. Bad ones.

"Osiris has compelled Skye to take her own life if she ever steps off the property, whether willingly or not." The words were uttered without emotion, but his nostrils flared at the end.

"Do you have one in mind?" Caro asked, her bright gaze on the child in his arms.

He considered and nodded. "I do."

"Share." A demand, not a request.

His lips curled at the impatience in her tone. Already his Caro was back to the angel he adored.

"*Anastasia* means 'resurrection' in ancient Greek, but it's far too plain for her." He brushed his knuckles down her neck to the blanket cocooning her tiny form. So soft. "How do you feel about Astasiya?" He didn't ask Caro, but his daughter. "A variation of Anastasia, but unique and empowering, and beautiful."

Delight tugged at his heart, confirming his choice.

"She approves," Caro murmured. "As do I. We can call her Stas for short."

"Is it common for Seraphim to perform a blood bond?"

She shook her head. "No. It only happens when the Fates dictate it as necessary, and occasionally…" She drifted off, her gaze leaving his for the wall. "Seraphim seldom join unless there is a rationale for it, but I've heard of a few who bonded because they wanted to."

"For love," he translated.

Her pupils dilated. "Yes. As you can imagine, it's frowned upon, but it has happened."

"Once you form the bond, can you tie yourself to anyone else?"

Her irises lit with a fire as her attention shifted back to him. "No. That would defeat the purpose of joining in blood."

Hence why she stated it would be eternal. He studied her angelic features, so fragile in appearance but underlined with a ferocity he adored. A warrior masked under a sea of beauty. The perfect mate. The mother of his child. The woman who owned his future.

"A commitment of eternity," he whispered.

"Yes."

"That's a lot to ask."

"As is the blood bond of a Seraphim," she returned.

Fair. It wasn't just his commitment but also hers. "We would be tied together forever, angel. You sure you want that?"

"I never offered."

His lips lifted at the edges, his voice soft. "Yes, Caro. You did."

"Tell me this is the right decision," she demanded. "Tell me."

"It's the only decision," he replied softly.

"Then why does it hurt so much?"

"Because we're sacrificing our hearts," he whispered. "For love."

She shook her head against him but said no more. Because there wasn't anything left to say or do. They could only endure what was to come. For Astasiya.

He held Caro and kissed her hair, her forehead, her temple, her eyes, and her lips. Memorizing every inch of the woman he'd grown to cherish and revere throughout the years. His mate. His other half. His partner in everything.

A few decades apart wouldn't kill them.

Astasiya would save them. As long as they moved this chess piece the right way.

"Eternity," Caro whispered.

"Eternity," he agreed, kissing her soundly.

"Ready?" he asked softly.

She shook her head, her little body shaking.

"They'll protect you, just like your parents did."

She bit her lip and eyed the home. "But Momma keeps talking to me. She needs help."

He grimaced in understanding. His mother, despite likely trying not to telegraph, kept sending agonizing images of her repeated deaths through the bond. It would dwindle as time went on, hopefully only pestering Astasiya in her dreams. If not, he would alter the rune on her back enough to help give her a semblance of peace.

"I'll search for your mom," he vowed. "While you live here, okay? And then one day, we'll go find her together."

"Promise?" she asked, those green eyes holding his with an intensity unusual for a seven-year-old.

"I vow it," he replied, squeezing her hand. "We'll find her."

"Together," she demanded.

"Together," he agreed. *When you're ready.*

ANGEL
BONDS

"*Vita mutatur, non tollitur,*" she read, tracing the inscription on the cover.

"Life is changed, not taken away," he translated. "I kept a journal for many years after Aidan turned me, and I thought you might want to have a piece of my past as you live through your present."

Her green eyes lifted, wonder turning her irises a luscious green. "You documented your first years as an immortal?"

"My first decades, yes." Men were often required to conceal strong emotions. He hid his in the form of a journal. "No one knows this exists except me, and now you."

He drew his finger along the old binding, the item one he hadn't touched in nearly two centuries until he wrapped it for her last week.

"There will be passages you may dislike," he warned. "But I never want to hide from you, Aya. And I want you to know that you can come to me with anything. No matter what happens, I'm here for you."

Tears gathered in her eyes as she held the notebook to her chest. "This is a beautiful gift, Issac."

Lizzie grabbed Jayson's wrist. "Just a bite."

His brow furrowed. "I thought you wanted me to eat the cookie."

"I do, but just try it first."

He appeared doubtful but did as she asked, and stared at the item in his hand. "It's pink."

She smiled. "I know."

Stas's lips curled down, not understanding why… *Oh.* Her eyes widened. *Oh!*

"But why would….?" His lips parted. "It's… it's…" His gaze misted with tears, his heart in his eyes. "Oh, it's a girl?"

She nodded. "Yes."

"Do you, Elizabeth, take Jayson to be yours forever, to love and to hold dear, from this day forward, for the rest of eternity and beyond?" Luc's voice carried across the beach, his position at the altar fitting.

"I do," Lizzie replied, her hands clasped in Jayson's palms, his smiling eyes holding hers. He hadn't stopped grinning since she appeared at the end of the aisle, had even shed a few tears at the sight of her walking toward him.

"And do you, Jayson, take Elizabeth to be yours forever, to love and to hold dear, from this day forward, for the rest of eternity and beyond?"

Adoration graced Jayson's features as he said, "Absolutely, I do."

"Allow me to lead, my lady." Issac held out his hand.

"Oh, is this the part where I call you *Your Highness*?" Stas recently learned about Issac's family ancestry. His father was a duke, making Issac the Duke of Wakefield after his father passed. Stas had yet to tease him about it, but now seemed as good a time as any.

"Technically, it's *Your Grace*, and no. You will not call me that."

"And if I do, Your Grace?" she asked, batting her eyelashes at him coquettishly.

He narrowed his gaze. "I'll be forced to punish you."

"This sounds enlightening. Please elaborate, Your Grace."

He looked her over, his stare assessing. "You want to play, darling?"

She smiled. "Always."

Stas stole a deep breath through her nose, focusing on the present, scanning her current surroundings.

Fatigues.

An army.

Sentinels.

Dotting the beach, running toward the party, firing their pistols without care for whom they hit.

"They're blocking us somehow!" Balthazar shouted.

"I know!" Issac returned from beside her.

A block?

Like a rune?

She frowned. Had Doctor Fitzgerald perfected the Sentinel technology enough to withstand Hydraian and Ichorian gifts?

"Aya…" God, she needed to breathe. Why wasn't her heart beating? He started the compressions again, needing to do something, *anything*. She couldn't be… No. He rejected it. This wasn't, *couldn't*, be. He just needed—

A hand on his shoulder jolted him. He stood and swung backward without thought, only to be caught in Balthazar's arms, unable to move, unable to fight, his chest heaving with the exertion.

"She's gone, Issac."

"Fuck you," he growled, fighting him, needing to go back to her, to save her, to—

"There's nothing you can do. She's gone."

Issac rejected the words, his fists swinging, Balthazar taking the hits and continuing to hold him.

"I'm sorry," he whispered. "I'm so sorry, Issac." Balthazar kept repeating the words, but Issac refused to hear them.

It felt *wrong*. Too soon.

"She can't be dead," he cried, collapsing to his knees again. "Balthazar, tell me she's not dead."

"I can't do that," Balthazar whispered, having followed Issac to the ground. "I wish I could, but I can't. She's gone."

"You would have liked it here, Aya," Issac murmured, his gaze on the stars above her grave. "It's been a while since I visited—perhaps a decade ago? We try to keep our presence here quiet, to not draw attention to ourselves for obvious reasons. Amazing what an annual contribution to charities will do to keep the public satisfied."

He took another fortifying sip of his—he eyed the label—whiskey. Ugh, he'd clearly hit rock bottom if this was all he had left of his stash. But he couldn't seem to drink the liquor fast enough.

"I want to feel numb, you see." He took another sip. "But this shite isn't doing it, darling. It's just burning my throat and insides at this point." He couldn't remember the last time he imbibed such copious amounts of alcohol. Perhaps after he turned Tristan? The two had gone on a drinking binge for entertainment purposes. It ended in a tangle of blondes.

Issac snorted. "That's not happening again. Ever." Another drink, followed by a sigh. The ground was cold beneath his jacket. Dead. Because it contained all his loved ones—Aidan, Mum, Aya.

"Fuck, I miss you," he whispered, his chest aching. "I miss all of you."

"I'm trying to find out where your brother buried Stas," he replied, glancing at her. "But he's being stubborn."

"What do you plan to do with the information?" Lucian asked.

"Dig up her grave and set her free. Otherwise, she'll just continue to cry in my head." Gabriel pinned Issac with a look. "Considering you're nearly bonded to her, I'm surprised you can't sense her."

His brow furrowed. "What?"

"He doesn't understand bonds," Ezekiel replied shortly. "As I've mentioned several times over, they're all ignorant when it comes to Seraphim. If you would just take five minutes to explain, perhaps they would be more willing to assist."

"Stas is a Seraphim." Lucian again. "And you're suggesting she's alive."

"I don't deal in suggestions, only facts," Stark clarified. "Now, where is she?"

Issac's heart skipped a beat.

This had to be a trick.

Astasiya's wings were the most marvelous sight of Issac's existence. He couldn't stop touching them, his fingers gliding over the silky texture, completely awed by her absolute beauty.

Her nails bit into the back of his neck as she pulled him in for another kiss. He was helpless to stop her, his need far too great for him to consider any alternative.

Fuck, he'd missed this. The ability to take her the way he desired, to slide his tongue into her mouth without worrying about the repercussions. Mmm, she tasted so good, like his favorite dream only sweeter and more alluring. He deepened the embrace, taking charge on instinct alone.

Her throaty purr of approval went straight to his groin, his body on fire for her. He undulated his hips into hers to provoke the sound from her once more and smiled when she added his name to the mix.

"More." She sank her teeth into his lower lip, her reprimand clear.

"Persuade me," he dared, returning her bite with one of his own. "Tell me what to do to you, Aya." He wanted to feel her power, to luxuriate in the reality that they could do whatever they desired without consequence. Because her blood wasn't toxic to him.

According to Gabriel.

It might be a lie.

So what if it is?

He held her close, his mouth and body worshipping hers as his name fell from her lips on a benediction that went straight to his heart.

Her fingers wove through his hair, her eyes glazed as he pulled back to kiss her. It grew into a war of tongues, blood, and ardor between them. Each touch, each thrust, each lick and nip, all intertwined to carry them into a future of *always*.

"Never stop," Astasiya whispered, her wings folded around them, cocooning them in a halo of pale feathers. "I never want to stop."

Issac grinned against her mouth. "Then we won't."

"I need…" Her lips trailed across his jaw, her tongue laving the column of his throat. "I want…" Her teeth grazed his skin, stirring a shiver from his soul.

Fate whispered foreign intentions into his ear, his heart skipping a beat. They weren't so much words as they were instincts, a knowledge founded on a plane of existence he didn't comprehend. But the pull took them under, Astasiya's incisors puncturing his skin, his blood flowing into her moaning mouth.

It burned in the most delicious way, catapulting him over the edge into oblivion.

"Aya," he groaned, pleasure quaking throughout him, his orgasm stealing the breath from his lungs. His hand fell between them, needing her to join him, but she was already there, her body shaking on top of his, her feathers rustling across the sheets.

His breath caught at the beauty of the moment.

The shimmering colors, blinking in and out, her long waves of blonde hair cascading across her shoulders. And the sense of rightness overwhelming them both.

"Ah, well, one day Ezekiel will truly heel. I just have to finish breaking him first."

"And my father?" Stas asked, folding her arms. "Is that what you're doing with him?"

His green eyes flickered beneath the lights, his lips flattening. "Sethios is a lost cause. You, however, I have hope for. And knowing you bonded to Issac has provided me with the most delicious training module."

How does he know about our blood bond? she wondered, shocked. *Is it something Seraphim can sense?*

That, or someone told him, Issac thought back at her, his tone underlined in fury. *My suspicion is it's the latter.*

Which means he might not know for sure…

"I'm not sure how much use I'll be to you," she said, an idea forming as she uttered each word. "I can't even figure out how to mist."

He gave her an indulgent smile. "You're still young. A baby, really. I'll teach you what you need to know." He shifted his focus to the cell beside her. "The offer stands for you as well. I've always been impressed by you and your practical stance on life. There's a future here, if you desire it."

"Assuming I can earn that future," Issac added, his tone calm. "Betrayal is hard to overcome."

"It is, yes," Osiris agreed. "That you even acknowledge that fact proves my point. You're valuable." He glanced around, his lips curling into one of his charming grins that made her queasy inside. "You all are, actually. We'll come to an understanding over the next few centuries. I'm certain of it."

"Ah, you impress me, Stas. Breaking your fight will be my biggest achievement." He petted her hair, cooing her name. "You'll be my most impressive—" He jolted backward, his focus shifting to the side. "*Vera,*" he growled.

"Hello, darling." A Seraphim with navy wings appeared, her smile radiant. "You really should pick on an angel your own age." She tsked. "Poor form."

He collapsed, a sound of pure rage ripping from his throat. "I'll—" The words died as he rolled to his back, his wings disappearing and his eyes falling closed.

"Well, that was easier than I expected," Vera said. "You exhausted him for me, Stas. Well done."

Stas couldn't reply, her own fatigue taking over. She had no concept of time or space or even what had just happened.

"He buried him two miles that way," Vera said, pointing through the trees. "Look for the fresh grave at the base of the mountain. Beneath the dirt is a cement tomb. But hurry, Gabriel. I can't hold Osiris for long." Her head fell back on a shudder, power rippling through the air around her. "And Skye…" She rolled her neck, her voice hollowing. "The lake, near the docks. There's not enough time—"

"Go," Stark said, his voice oddly close but far away.

"But Sethios—" That sounded like Ezekiel.

"Issac and I will handle it," Stark interjected. "Save Skye."

You're my always, Aya, he whispered, hugging her to him. *Whatever you need, I'm here. Wherever you go, I'll go. We're a team, you and I. No matter the obstacle, no matter the trial, I will never leave your side. That's my vow to you, always and forever. Across the universe and beyond, I will love you.*

She remained quiet for so long that he thought perhaps she'd fallen asleep. But then she asked, *Why does that feel like a proposal?*

He smiled. *It's not.*

Oh. She almost sounded disappointed.

It's my wedding vow, he whispered. *During Elizabeth and Jayson's ceremony, I couldn't stop thinking about what I would say to you, how I would convey my feelings. And the words just came to me, the certainty in them completing me in a way that just felt right. I'd intended to say them to you that night. I didn't get a chance, so I'm saying them now.*

She rolled in his arms, her tired gaze finding his as she cupped his cheek.

"You're my always, Issac," she said, her voice soft yet clear. "I promise to honor you, to cherish you, to be honest with you, and to respect you. To work with you, not against you. To forever remain by your side, regardless of the trial or task. And to trust you, always and forever. Across the universe and beyond, I will love you."

Emotion burned in his eyes, his throat thickening as he whispered, "Always."

"Always," she replied. *You may now kiss the bride,* she added in his mind, causing him to grin.

The perfect wedding, he whispered to her.

To the perfect man, she agreed. *My always.*

My always, he repeated, his lips claiming hers. *I love you, Aya.*

I love you, too.

Bahal
02/11

Astasiya stood outside, her face tilted back to enjoy the sun blazing overhead. She kept flickering in and out of her ethereal state, her gorgeous wings flaring around her and disappearing and flaring again. Her childlike smile said it was on purpose.

"She's finally figured out how to mist," Issac murmured, joining him at the sliding glass door. "She wants to visit Elizabeth first."

"Her friend, right?" Sethios asked, recalling the name from Leela's rundown about Astasiya's current life. "She's pregnant?"

Issac nodded. "Yes. I don't think she's due for another month, but it's all very strange. Leela seems to have it handled."

"She would. She helped Caro birth Astasiya as well." He studied his daughter's excited expression. "I need to find Caro."

"And you want Astasiya's help," the intuitive male beside him surmised, his intelligence somewhat respectable.

"Yes."

"Then tell her," he replied, making it sound like the simplest task in the world.

"How?"

It felt weird asking another man how to talk to his own daughter, but these weren't normal circumstances. And after everything Sethios had endured, he wasn't quite sure how to talk to anyone, let alone his own flesh and blood.

"By being honest and forthright." He faced him. "She's still a bit miffed over being left in the dark all these years. The truth will go a long way."

"What I mean to say is, working together—as a team—is the only way we'll locate your mother. Because I know, without a doubt, that my father has hidden her somewhere difficult and impossible to find. But I've left your mother to suffer for—"

"Dad," she interjected, the single word a caress against his frozen heart. "You don't need to explain. I want to find her, too."

Oh. Right. "Have I mentioned how much you remind me of your mother?"

"A few times." She smiled, her expression even more reminiscent of Caro. "When do we leave?"

He studied her. "As soon as possible."

"Good." She took a step back. "Then I'd better perfect the art of misting." Her wings appeared. "I'll be right back." She vanished, causing him to shake his head.

You'd be so proud of her, Caro, he thought, smiling. *She's just as brave and as fearless as you.*

Nothing.

His shoulders fell, his eyes falling closed. *Come back to me, darling. I miss you.*

He took a step, his soul weeping inside, when a distant whisper prickled the back of his thoughts.

The words were faint, as if carried on a breeze.

Free me, Sethios…

Free.

Me.

Babelar
25/10/20

Seraphim do not feel.

Seraphim do not love.

Seraphim do not react.

Those are the rules every higher being lives by.

And Caro broke them all for *him*.

Now she's lost in a vacant sea, punished for the ultimate sin of choosing an abomination—*a vampire*—over her duty.

Sethios promised to come for her, to find her, to save her, but with each passing breath, her hope melts into despair.

Will he find her in time? Or will her mind shatter from the madness?

Welcome to the Immortal Curse world.

The High Council of Seraph will see you now…

Sethios and Caro will return in Blood Seeker…

An unexpected connection led to a forbidden affair that ended in blood. Now Sethios will stop at nothing to find his mate, even if it means risking his life and love in the process.

Caro's mind is fractured, her body destroyed, her heart broken. She thought he would come for her, save her, free her from this nightmare. But her hope flees with every wave, her soul teetering on the brink of madness.

Will Sethios arrive in time? Or will other powers intervene?

A new prophecy is rising… One that will threaten to destroy them all.

Immortal Curse World

Bonus Stories & Fun Extras
Set Within the
Immortal Curse World

ELDER
BONDS

A Collection of Immortal Curse Stories
Such as the day Luc met B...

"A sensual talent?" Balthazar murmured. "Tell me more."

Ah, so the mind-reading bit was true. "I'd rather show you." He held out his hand. "Lucian."

"Balthazar." The male accepted the welcoming gesture while holding Luc's gaze intently. "Your mind is intoxicating."

"The one brooding in the corner," Balthazar murmured. "He's useful."

Luc followed his gaze to a young male with long brown hair. He had a knee drawn up to his chest and the opposite leg stretched out along the ground. The immortal beside him appeared to be trying to make small talk—unsuccessfully.

"He's telepathic and claimed his other gift to be linguistics," B continued. "But that's not all he can do."

Dark brown eyes lifted to them—sensing their interest—and narrowed.

Balthazar smiled. "Extremely useful."

"He doesn't seem too eager."

"Leave that part to me," B replied, his focus shifting. "We need that one too." He nodded toward another dark-haired man, this one grinning at the nearby sentry. "He's new—only a few weeks into his immortality—but he grew up here. His father apparently tried to kill him a few times and told Osiris. That's the reason we're all here."

"Why is he smiling?" Luc wondered, frowning. The man looked almost happy to be here.

"He's taunting the guard, and it's working. They know each other."

Hello, gorgeous. Alik sent the telepathic message to the curvy blonde dancing in the waves a few yards away. She flung out her arms and spun in a circle as fire flickered across her fingertips.

His lips curled in amusement. Jenika always did this after battle. It was the adrenaline rush from engaging her pyrokinesis that left her exuberant and smiling. Even covered in blood, she looked radiant and full of life.

He admired her exposed legs as she pulled her white shift over her head, tossing it into the ocean. All that long, silky hair flowed down her naked back as she whirled an intoxicating mix of water and flames.

Alik had never seen someone so beautiful. He lounged on the black sand—legs stretched out and crossed at the ankles—and supported his upper body on his elbows.

Dance for me, he whispered seductively into her mind.

Her hazel eyes glimmered with arousal as she moved in a way that drove him wild. The water only reached her thighs, leaving everything on display for his open perusal. So fucking sexy.

Power rippled out of him, directed at the redheaded bitch. He put everything he had into that mental punch, all his pain and agony, and tripled it inside her mind.

The air around him cooled immediately. Third-degree burns lined every inch of his being, the salt water around him only worsening the condition, and yet, he felt nothing.

No pain.

No torment.

He'd pushed it all out and into the redheaded Ichorian writhing on the ground.

I'm empty.

Others came spilling onto the sand beyond her, all of them wielding various powers he knew nothing about. He didn't care who they were or where they came from. Just touched all their minds. Every. Single. One. And spread the torture rampant.

Everyone fell to their knees.

Agonized yells littered the beach.

Alik stepped out of the ocean, his legs shaking with the effort. And yet, his mind felt fine. He searched out all the intruders on the island, over a hundred of them, and sent shock waves of his dangerous gift through all of them.

Die…

"Sorry, old friend. But it's the only way."

What?

The muzzle flashed before Eli could even think to react.

Amelia!

Oh, shit. Oh, holy shit. No…This…What the fuck just happened?!

His heart ached, his breath leaving on a sharp gasp. No. This couldn't be real. A nightmare. How many millennia had he lived? How many centuries with his Amelia? Protecting her, loving her, cherishing her…

To go down like this? To fail her?

Amelia…

His head dropped, his vision blackening.

Not like this.

A dark hole whirled around him, different from all the other times he'd died. He usually fell into a state of unconsciousness and awoke later as if from a dream. But this wasn't right.

Her fingers clutched his as the last vestiges of reality left him on a whoosh of air.

My final breath.

"Don't stop playing with me now," Balthazar murmured. "We were just getting started."

"I don't believe we were doing anything."

"And that's a shame, isn't it? Two beautiful people, lounging on a romantic beach, just chatting?" He held out his hand. "Balthazar. You can call me B."

She eyed his strong fingers, attached to a leanly muscled arm.

What could it hurt? She had to wipe his memory anyway. Might as well enjoy the moment.

Electricity hummed between them as she pressed her palm to his. "Leela. You can call me Lee."

"Lee," he repeated, as if tasting the word. "And if I prefer Leela?"

She shrugged. "Then I'll call you Balthazar."

Sexy dimples appeared. "You can call me whatever you like."

"Amazing," he whispered in between her demanding kisses. "Fucking amazing."

He let go. Stopped worrying. Just enjoyed and yielded to his needs. It was intoxicating, dangerous, and so damn good. They came together, her moans mingling with his, their bodies slick with sweat. His forehead met hers, his breathing rapid, her chest heaving, and still he craved more.

"Again," she demanded. "It shouldn't be possible, but again."

"Yes." He lifted her, his direction the bedroom. "All night."

"And morning."

"All weekend."

Leela nodded, her lips brushing his as she gulped in air. "Take me, B."

He lowered her onto his bed, their bodies still joined. "With pleasure, love."

"I can't believe you made me go through every floor." She shivered while her demon chuckled.

"Full experience, remember?"

"One I could live without."

"It's all glamour, darling." His lips curled into one of his trademark sinful smiles. "I still can't believe all of those things frighten you, but Osiris does not."

"Oh, he scares the shit out of me. I face him out of necessity. That"—she pointed to the stairwell they'd just escaped from—"is pointless horror that causes heart attacks for no viable reason."

"You don't approve of my theatrics?" a sensual voice asked from up ahead. "Perhaps you should take her to level thirteen, Wakefield. Might be more her speed."

Stas met Balthazar's warm gaze and cocked a brow. "Is it more blood and gore?"

"Only for those requesting it," he murmured, a sinful note to his tone. The Hydraian Elder oozed sexual energy, even now, in a darkly lit hallway leading to who the fuck knew where. "The heart of the party, sweetheart."

HAPPY
HALLOWEEN

Welcome to the Immortal Curse world, where angels and vampires live in secret… for now.

Gabriel is a warrior. A Seraphim. An immortal of astute power and authority. He's lived his life beneath a cloud of stoicism and practicality. Only to have his entire existence turned over on its head because of *her*.

Clara. The witch who enchanted him with her empathy—a vampiric talent wreaking havoc on his ability to focus.

He's hell-bent on righting the wrong, even if it means killing her to restore his mental sensibilities.

However, not all battles are fought physically.

Some require heart.

Clara's no normal adversary.

And she's about to bring Gabriel to his knees.

Author's Note: This episodic novella is part of the Immortal Curse world and best enjoyed when read as a companion story to the Immortal Curse series. Begin the journey today with *Blood Laws.*

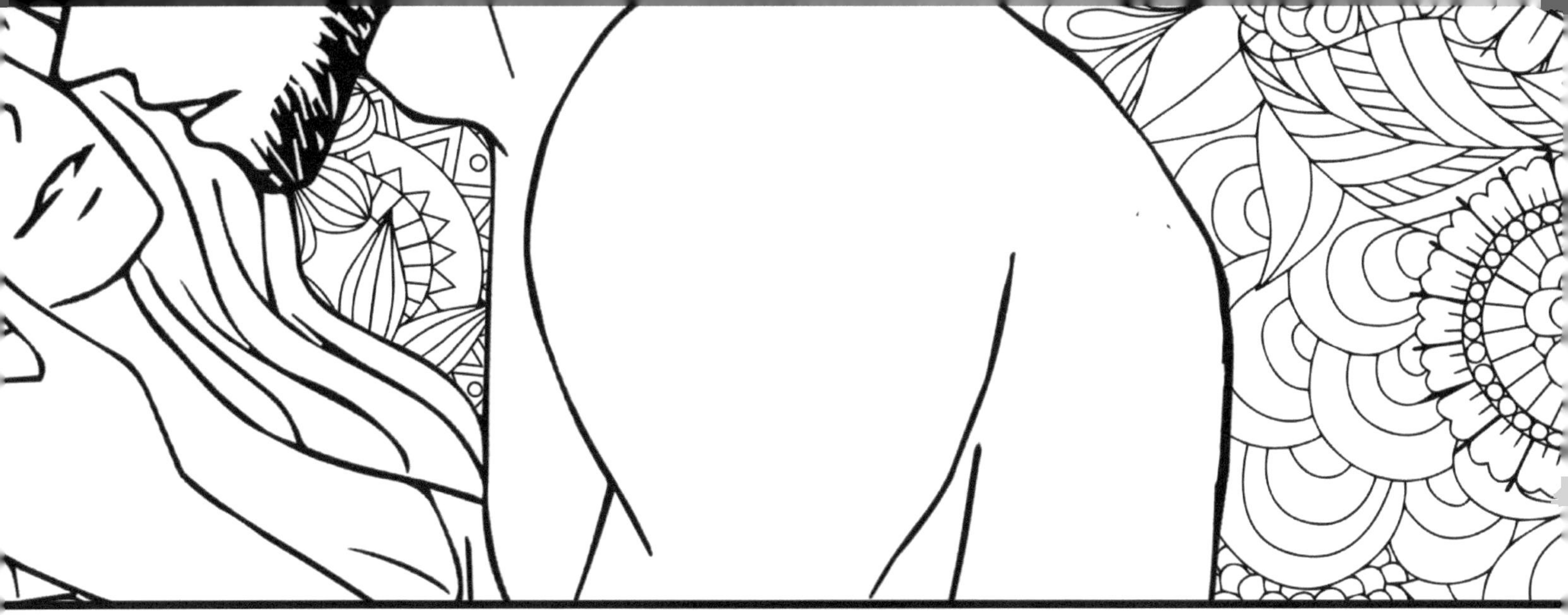

DON'T MISS

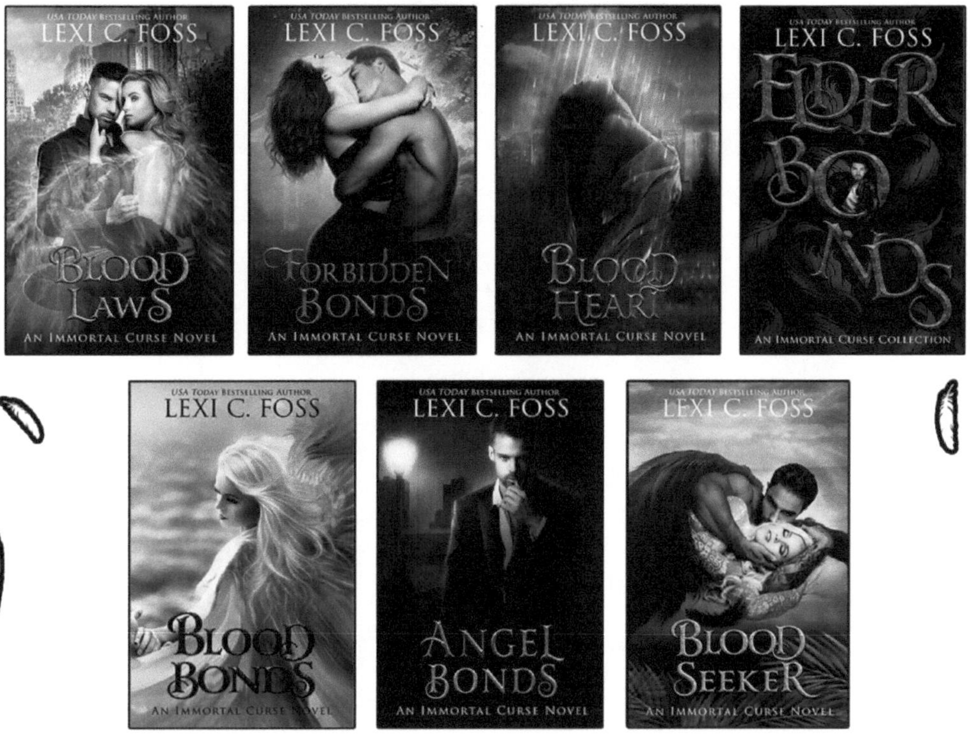
LEXI C. FOSS
BLOOD LAWS
AN IMMORTAL CURSE NOVEL
LEXI C. FOSS
FORBIDDEN BONDS
AN IMMORTAL CURSE NOVEL
LEXI C. FOSS
BLOOD HEART
AN IMMORTAL CURSE NOVEL
LEXI C. FOSS
ELDER BONDS
AN IMMORTAL CURSE COLLECTION
LEXI C. FOSS
BLOOD BONDS
AN IMMORTAL CURSE NOVEL
LEXI C. FOSS
ANGEL BONDS
AN IMMORTAL CURSE NOVEL
LEXI C. FOSS
BLOOD SEEKER
AN IMMORTAL CURSE NOVEL

IMMORTAL
CURSE
SERIES

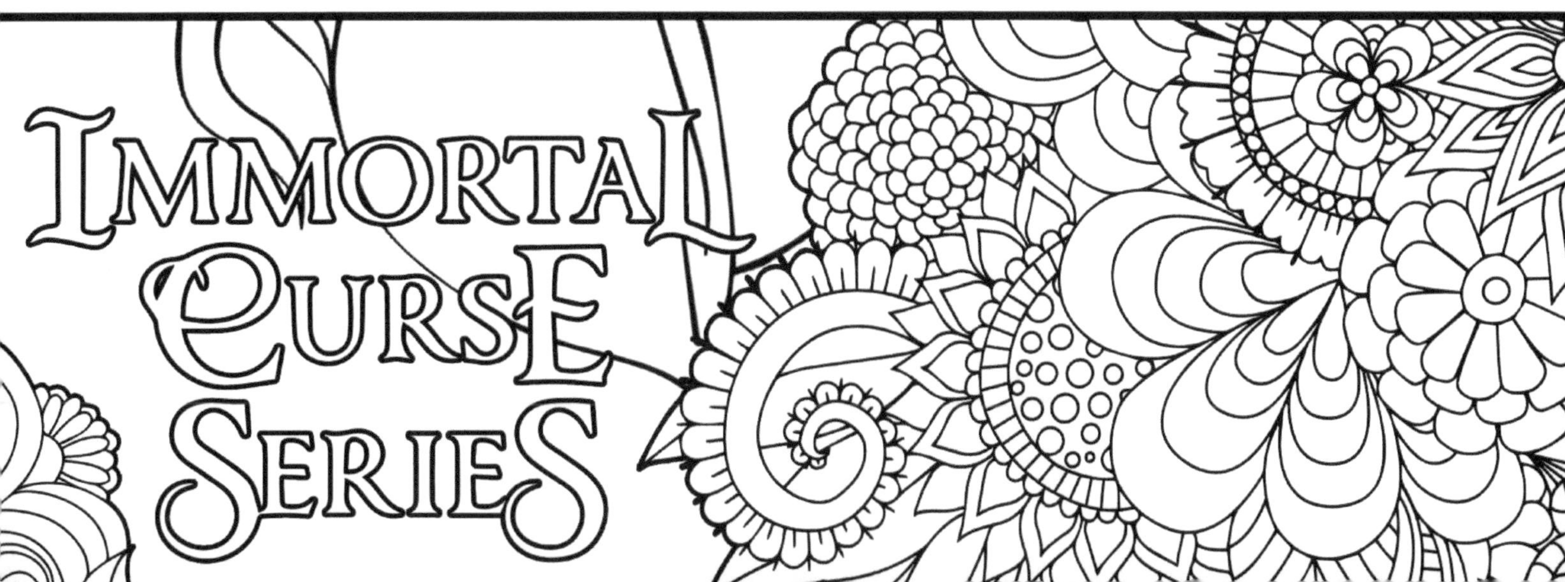